W9-CCR-922

A New True Book

THE PAWNEE

By Dennis B. Fradin

CHILDRENS PRESS ®

CHICAGO

A Pawnee dancer

PHOTO CREDITS

© Jim Argo—4, 15 (left), 21 (left), 25 (2 photos), 38, 39 (2 photos), 40, 41 (3 photos), 42 (2 photos), 43 (2 photos), 44 (2 photos), 45 (2 photos)

© Reinhard Brucker—9, 13, 15 (middle and right), 18 (left), 19 (2 photos), 21 (right), 27 (2 photos), 29 (2 photos)

© Jerry Hennen—7

Museum of the American Indian, Heye Foundation—23 (2 photos)

National Museum of American Art, Smithsonian Institution—16, 30

© Photri—18 (right)

© Chris Roberts—Cover, 2

© H. Armstrong Roberts—33

Warner Collection of Gulf States Paper Corporation, Tuscaloosa, AL—35

Western History Collections, University of Oklahoma Library—11, 37

Al Magnus—7 (map)
Cover—Pawnee dancer, Bill McClelland

For their help, the author thanks:

Phyllis Gonzales, member, Pawnee tribe

Harrison Fields, Executive Director, Pawnee Tribe, Pawnee, Oklahoma

Library of Congress Cataloging-in-Publication Data

Fradin, Dennis B.
  The Pawnee / by Dennis B. Fradin.
    p.   cm. — (A New true book)
  Includes index.
  Summary: Describes the history, beliefs, customs, homes, and day-to-day life of the Pawnee Indians. Also discusses their present-day status.
  ISBN 0-516-01155-3
  1. Pawnee Indians—Juvenile literature. 2. Indians of North America—Great Plains—Juvenile literature. [1. Pawnee Indians. 2. Indians of North America—Great Plains.] I. Title
E99.P3F68 1988   88-11820
978'.00497—dc19   CIP
                                   AC

Childrens Press®, Chicago
Copyright ©1988 by Regensteiner Publishing Enterprises, Inc.
All rights reserved. Published simultaneously in Canada.
Printed in the United States of America.
    6 7 8 9 10 R 00 99 98 97 96

TABLE OF CONTENTS

EARLY PAWNEE HISTORY

Today, there are only about three thousand Pawnee. Most of them live in Oklahoma. But hundreds of years ago, the Pawnee were a mighty tribe with many thousands of people.

It's a mystery where the Pawnee first lived. Some people believe they came from somewhere in what is now the southern United States. They say that the Pawnee settled in Nebraska more than five hundred years ago.

The Pawnee say they were always there.

The Pawnee called themselves the *Chahiksichakihs*, meaning "Men of Men." Some other Native Americans called them the *Pawnee*. When Europeans came, they also used the name Pawnee— the name by which they are known today.

THE LAND SHAPED
THEIR WAY OF LIFE

Nebraska, where the
Pawnee lived for so long,
is rather flat. It is part of a
huge, flat area called
the *Great Plains*. Because
no tall mountains block the

7

sky, the stars are very
lovely over Nebraska
at night.

Nebraska has rich soil
that is good for farming.
It has vast grasslands,
where millions of buffalo
once roamed.

The Pawnee built their
villages near rivers so that
they could obtain water for
drinking and wood for fires.
They farmed the rich
soil near the rivers. They
hunted buffalo on the
grasslands. And, because

This Pawnee star chart, made on rawhide, shows the position of the stars in the sky.

the stars were so beautiful over their homeland, they developed many customs having to do with astronomy.

9

PAWNEE VILLAGES

The Pawnee were
divided into four bands, or
groups. The four were the
Chaui, Kitkehahki,
Pitahauerat, and Skidi.
Each band had its own
villages. By 1859 most
villages were located in
eastern Nebraska. A few
were in northern Kansas.

The Pawnee lived in
round houses called *earth
lodges*, made of dirt and

A Pawnee family proudly stands in front of their earth lodge.

grasses supported by wooden posts. The Pawnee used the round shape because they wanted their lodges to look like the dome of the sky.

The typical Pawnee

village had between ten and twelve earth lodges. About eight families lived in each lodge, amounting to about forty people. The entire village might have about 400 or 500 people.

For eight months of the year the Pawnee traveled in search of buffalo and other game. But they returned to their villages at planting time in spring and at harvest time in autumn.

HOW THEY DIVIDED THEIR WORK

Like other American Indians, the Pawnee divided their work between men and women. The women farmed. They grew corn, squash, and beans. Corn was so important that the

Saddles and hoes were carved from buffalo bones. The saddle made travel and hunting easier. The hoe was an important farming tool.

Pawnee called it *atira*, meaning "mother."

The women also did the cooking. It took teamwork to cook two meals a day for forty people. One meal was prepared by the women on the north side of the lodge. The other was made by the women on the south side. The women also made bowls, spoons, and other household items. And the women, especially the

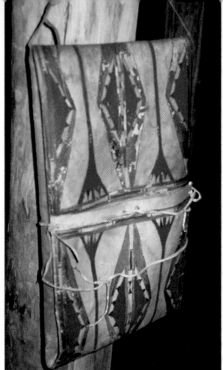

The Pawnee decorated their clothing and household items with colorful feathers, beads, and paint.

grandmothers, did most of the child raising.

The men made bows and arrows and other weapons. They hunted deer, elk, and antelope. Twice a year the men went on buffalo hunts.

Buffalo Bull,
a Pawnee
painted by George
Catlin in 1832,
wears an image
of the buffalo painted
on his chest and face.

Some men also served
as the *chiefs*, or leaders,
and as the *medicine men*,
or religious leaders. And
when the Pawnee went
to war, the men did the
fighting.

THE IMPORTANCE OF THE BUFFALO

The two yearly buffalo hunts—one in summer and the other in winter—were very important. The men did the hunting, but nearly everyone from the village traveled with the hunters. Away from home, the Pawnee lived in tents called *tipis*.

The buffalo provided many items for the Pawnee.

Some buffalo weighed a thousand
pounds or more. Buffalo skins were used
to make tipis (right).

The people ate the meat.
They used the skins to
make robes, blankets, and
tipis. From the buffalo
sinews (tendons) they made
thread and bowstrings.
Buffalo hair was braided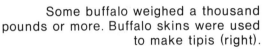
into rope, horns were

Buffalo altar (left) and
hide painting (right)
of a Pawnee battle

made into spoons, and
buffalo shoulder blades
became hoes.

The Pawnee believed the
buffalo was a special gift
sent them by the spirits.
They had ceremonies to
thank the spirits for sending
the buffalo.

WHAT THE PAWNEE BELIEVED

The Pawnee believed in a main spirit, Tirawa, who had created the Earth and the heavenly bodies. Many of the bright stars and planets made by Tirawa were considered gods. Four bright star-gods were believed to hold up the heavens.

Two of Tirawa's creations were the Morning Star (a man) and the

Stars have an important place in Pawnee life. They were painted on most of their items. Today, the star appears on the great seal of the Pawnee nation (left).

Evening Star (a woman). Long ago, the Pawnee said, the Evening Star and the Morning Star mated. They produced the first person, a little girl. She was carried down to Earth from the heavens by a whirlwind. Soon after that, the Sun mated with the Moon to create the first boy, who was also carried to Earth.

The Pawnee believed that, after their people died, they went to live with Tirawa in the sky. To reach Tirawa's home, the dead spirits followed a path along the Milky Way.

The Pawnee had many other customs and beliefs associated with heavenly bodies. When they saw two twinkling stars in a

Woman's buckskin dress (left) and man's shirt (right) were worn during a special religious rite called the Ghost Dance.

certain position in the sky, they held the spring ceremony. When they saw shooting stars, they thought it meant their enemies were coming to attack. And when the

23

harvest star (the star Canopus) appeared in the sky, they knew it was time to gather their crops.

To thank Tirawa and the stars, the Pawnee held religious ceremonies. They believed that by performing ceremonies they made sure the Earth would continue to provide food. One ceremony was held at corn-planting time. There were also ceremonies when it came time to harvest the corn and hunt the buffalo.

THE LIFE OF
PAWNEE CHILDREN

Children usually lived
with their mothers, but not
always with their fathers. A
Pawnee man could be
married to several women
at once. This meant that a

child's father might live
in a different lodge.
But wherever they lived,
fathers provided their
children with food and
other necessities.

Pawnee children treated
their parents with great
respect. The relationship
was much closer with
grandparents. Grandmothers
saw to the children's daily
needs, and gave them
special treats and toys.

Grandfathers played
games with the children

Soon after children left their cradle boards (right), they played with toys like the ones pictured above: a sled, doll, horse, and tipi.

and joked with them.
One popular trick of the
grandfathers was to
dump their grandsons
in the snow or into a
cold stream in the
morning. This was
supposed to harden the
boys for future life.

Young girls and boys worked in the lodge and out in the fields. Girls stayed home until they married (about age fifteen). But at age ten or so, some boys went to live in the lodges of their mothers' brothers. The uncles taught the boys how to hunt, fight, and make tools. Boys generally married when they were about eighteen years old.

WARFARE

The Pawnee were often
at war with other tribes.
The Cheyenne and the
Sioux were among their
main enemies. Generally
the American Indians made
surprise attacks, called raids.

Pawnee war shield (left) and war shirt (right)

Buffalo Chase with Bows and Lances, painting by George Catlin, 1830-1839

For about seven months each year, the Pawnee were away from their villages hunting buffalo. Only a few sick, old, and very young people stayed in the villages. The Pawnee's enemies often chose those times to

attack. They entered
villages on horseback,
killed people, stole horses,
wrecked the lodges, and
destroyed the crops.

One time 600 Sioux
approached a Pawnee
village, ready to attack. A
Pawnee named Crooked
Hand left his sickbed and
organized the elders,
children, and sick men
into a fighting force. The
Sioux were said to have
laughed when they saw

the children with their little
bows and the sick and
elderly people who came
out to fight them. But
Crooked Hand's forces
fought so fiercely that
the Sioux soon fled.

The Pawnee also raided
enemy villages. They killed
some of their foes.
However, the main purpose
of most Pawnee raids was
not to kill people. Usually,
the Pawnee wanted to
steal horses.

Coronado explored the southwestern United States.

THE PAWNEE LOSE THEIR LANDS

In 1541 the Spanish explorer Francisco Vásquez de Coronado entered the Pawnee land. This was the first meeting between the Pawnee and European people.

The Spanish explorers brought the first horses to America. The Pawnee captured some of the Spanish horses. The Pawnee came to value horses highly.

The Pawnee had little trouble with the white settlers for several hundred years. Then in the mid-1800s American settlers wanted to cross through Pawnee lands on their way west. The Pawnee let them.

Soon, though, the settlers did not want just to *pass through* Pawnee lands. They wanted the lands for themselves. The United States government forced the Pawnee to sell most of

Petalesharo, a famous Pawnee, visited Washington, D.C., in 1821.

This drawing of the Pawnee (above) was made by Samuel Seymour in 1819. It shows Pawnee meeting with a U.S. government official.

their Nebraska lands. They did this by tricking the Pawnee and by supplying their enemies with weapons. In 1857 the Pawnee were placed on a *reservation* near Genoa, Nebraska.

Pawnee scouts
in 1869

On the reservation the
Pawnee died in large
numbers from diseases.
When the settlers decided
that they wanted all the
Pawnee lands in Nebraska,
the Pawnee were powerless.

By 1875, the Pawnee
had been forced to move to
a reservation in Oklahoma.

The chief of police of the Pawnee

THE PAWNEE TODAY

Today the Pawnee are
scattered across about
thirty states. More of them
live in and near the town
of Pawnee, Oklahoma, than
anywhere else. This is where

Pawnee courthouse (left) and health center (above)

the Pawnee settled when
they were forced from
Nebraska over a century
ago. The Pawnee tribal
government is located here.

Drummers concentrate on their song during a Memorial Day powwow.

In many ways, the
Pawnee live and dress like
other Americans. Quite
a few of them work in
government jobs or in
factories. The Pawnee also
work as teachers, secretaries,
nurses, storekeepers, and
accountants.

Many Pawnee work for the tribe as teachers, council members, and hospital aides.

Some Pawnee have last names, such as Horse Chief, Sun Eagle, and Good Chief. Many of the elders speak the Pawnee language as well as English, and many of the young people

A hospital worker (left) and government worker (right)

know at least a few
Pawnee words. The elders
hand down stories about
their people to the young
ones, as the Pawnee have
done for hundreds of years.

Each summer, Pawnee
people from all over the
United States gather at
Pawnee, Oklahoma. They
dress in the traditional
clothes, dance the tribal
dances, and play Pawnee

World War II veteran (left);
Pawnee Memorial Day princess (right)

games. "Homecoming" is a
time when the Pawnee
celebrate the fact that
they have survived as a
people since before the
first Europeans settled in
America.

WORDS YOU SHOULD KNOW

astronomy (uh • STRON • uh • mee) — the study of stars, planets, and other heavenly bodies

buffalo (BUFF • uh • low) — large animals that provided the Pawnee with meat, clothes, and other supplies

Chahiksichakihs — the Pawnee name for themselves, meaning "Men of Men"

chiefs (CHEEFS) — leaders

earth lodges (ERTH LAJ • iz) — round houses made of dirt, grasses, and wood

Evening Star (EEV • ning STAHR) — the Pawnee spirit of night

Great Plains (GRATE PLAYNES) — a huge, rather flat region of North America that includes Nebraska

medicine men (MED • ih • sin MEN) — religious leaders

Morning Star (MOR • ning • STAHR) — the Pawnee spirit of war, light, and fire

Pawnee (paw • NEE) — a tribe that lived for hundreds of years in Nebraska, and which now has its headquarters in Oklahoma

raids (RAYDZ) — surprise attacks

reservations (rez • er • VAY • shunz) — areas kept by the government for Native Americans

tipis (TEE • peez) — tents

Tirawa (tih • RAH • luah) — the main spirit of the Pawnee

INDEX

About the Author

Dennis Fradin attended Northwestern University on a partial creative scholarship and was graduated in 1967. His previous books include the Young People's Stories of Our States series for Childrens Press, and Bad Luck Tony for Prentice-Hall. In the True book series Dennis has written about astronomy, farming, comets, archaeology, movies, space colonies, the space lab, explorers, and pioneers. He is married and the father of three children.